The Cougar Artist Next Door

A Milf Age Gap Erotic Romance

By Sora Seider

To My Dear Readers—May You
Continue to Grow in Number

4

The summer after my sophomore year of college, I came home to find that we had new neighbors. The old owners of the house, a pair of doctors, had retired to Florida. I had never so much as said two words to either of them, so I can't say I was sad to see them go.

Furthermore, the couple who moved in was a private equity consultant, Mr. Mirbeau, and his gorgeous wife, a sculptor. They apparently had a single son, somewhat older than I was and estranged.

The first thing they did when they moved into their two-story town house was put one of Mrs. Mirbeau's sculptures in the front garden: a full, life-sized male figure, naked and fit, his arms thrown back as if about to accept a hug. Most controversial amongst the neighborhood mothers, however, was the statue's genitals: a massive, erect cock, easily visible to anyone who passed by. It was an exquisite piece, accurate to the tiniest detail. The neighborhood association tried to get her to take the statue down, or at least cover or remove the genitals, "for the children," as they say. Mrs. Mirbeau laughed in their faces; the statue stayed.

I can't blame Mrs. Mirbeau for sculpting the statue with an erect cock; I would be surprised, to be honest, if she has ever seen a flaccid one. She had a beautifully toned body that came from regular exercise, toned legs and a slim waist, but with a fullness at the chest and hips that lent her an exquisite hourglass figure. She had high cheeks, thick cherry lips, and long locks of curly black hair that fell about her pale face. It was painful even to look at her; I could only catch second-length glances before I had to turn away, lest my pants burst.

Her husband, for his part, was not nearly as attractive; not ugly, per se, but compared to his wife he seemed mediocre, his body out of shape, his face of unideal proportions. And supposedly he was an utterly charmless individual, and occasionally nasty to those who talked to him. One suspects she married him for his money; their sex life could not have been satisfactory for her (though for him, one imagines, it was heaven).

All this to say that, upon first glimpsing Mrs. Mirbeau as she walked to her car one evening on my first week back from college, I was entranced by everything about her. The sway of her hips, the movement of her body. (Also, of course, her art.) But I did not speak to her for a while, or catch more than brief glimpses of her in windows or as she went out walking. I did not seek her out; though I was fit, and have been told I was quite handsome with my chiseled body and intense dark eyes, I could not imagine that an older woman, especially one as gorgeous as Mrs. Mirbeau, would take any interest in me.

Needless to say, I was happy to discover how wrong I was.

The first sign of how wrong I was came on my second week back. I was in my bathroom one evening brushing my teeth before bed, dressed in nothing more than a Nirvana t-shirt and a pair of white boxers, when I spied something outside my window.

My bedroom and the attendant bathroom are on the second floor of our house, and the bathroom window looked out upon the side of the Mirbeau's house; from not too difficult an angle, one could view their carefully mown backyard and its maze of erotic statues, doubtless the creations of Mrs. Mirbeau. Occasionally I liked to lean around the window and look at them for a while.

8

But that evening, in the low dusk light, I saw something else, as well. A figure, with thigh-length curly black hair, sculpting. I could not see her face, for her back was to me, but I knew it to be Mrs. Mirbeau by circumstance and by her hair.

She moved; her hair swished in the breeze; I realized, breathlessly, that she was sculpting naked.

Without even thinking I had whipped my cock out and was urgently tugging it. I imagined the curve of her body, the smooth whiteness of her skin, how she would feel under me—

What she was working on, at that point, was not clay but a mess of wires she appeared to be gradually forming into the general shape of a human. It was life-size, a few inches taller than her.

She moved around, to work the wires on its back, and I saw the pale full moons of her breasts heave in the dusk light, as her curls swayed around them.

God, she was gorgeous.

I tugged more urgently at my cock. It was so stiff in my hand it was painful.

I desperately wanted something warm and soft and wet and tight to stuff it in.

Not just anything warm and soft and wet and tight—I wanted Mrs. Mirbeau's gorgeous pussy.

The sun had fully set by now, but the moon was as full as her breasts, and I could still see her clearly in the moonlight. Below the narrowing navel of her waist, in the cleft where her legs met, was a gorgeous bush of black hair.

I salivated. I wanted her so badly.

Watching her, I lost myself. I yelled as I came, my essence shooting out in a massive white wad that hit the window with a thud.

Nobody saw, but nonetheless I felt my cheeks grow hot.

What if my parents heard? I could just say I stubbed my toe. Clean up quickly, pull my boxers back on, and no one would be any the wiser.

But what if Mrs. Mirbeau looked up, saw me watching her like a pervert? Saw a white splotch on the window like a splatter of bird shit? Would she connect two and two together?

As if my worries had summoned her gaze, at that moment Mrs. Mirbeau looked away from her statue, directly at my window.

It was night; she was far away; but in the moonlight I could swear I saw her smile.

The next day I mulled over the smile, over my losing myself. I was embarrassed; I was anxious; I was also hopeful. Vague, in the back of my head, too delightful a possibility for me to dare utter: what if she saw and understood everything, and wanted me too?

My parents left at around 5:30 to have dinner with some family friends; I feigned sickness and begged to stay home. My musing throughout the day was easily interpretable as illness; they agreed.

At 6:00 pm, the doorbell rang.

It was Mrs. Mirbeau. Clothed, of course. Her clothes were casual, jeans and a plain white tucked-in t-shirt, each flecked with dried bits of clay and paint, but somehow she made it look stylish and sexy. It was like I wasn't looking at an artist in her dirty work clothes so much as at a model mimicking a stylized version of such an artist.

My mouth was dry. "Can I help you? Uh, Mrs. Mirbeau, right?"

She smiled. God, what a sexy smile. "Why yes, I believe you can.

Cameron, right? Please, call me Emily."

I nodded my assent.

Her eyes twinkled. "Well, Cameron, I noticed last night that you liked my little show. So I thought it only fair that you pay me back somehow. Would you mind modeling for me? I have my mesh cage ready for my next human figure, but I need a model to build off of."

"Uh, when were you thinking of having me model?"

"I was thinking right now, if you're free."

I tried desperately not to leap out the front door. Holy fuck. "I think I can do that. I don't have much going on tonight."

"Great. Come with me."

I let her take my hand. Her skin was warm and rough from working wire and clay. Somehow that roughness, even amongst all her other attributes, was the most erotic thing about her. More so than her figure or her hair or how she moved, or her smile. Feeling her hand in mine was like a little death. I let her lead me through my family's yard; through her own; through her house; and into her backyard. I barely registered any of it. Only her, just ahead of me, leading me by the hand, and the feeling of her warm rough palm against mine.

"Here we are. Now, I was hoping to have this sculpture be a nude. Could you take your clothes off?"

She had let go of my hand, was standing in front of me. We were surrounded by her creations, clay men and women with bodies of lithe, erotic grace, all entirely nude, caught as if in the midst of movement.

My cock was hard at the prospect of being naked in front of Mrs. Mirbeau—though she told me to call her Emily, I still cannot think of her as anything but Mrs. Mirbeau. Without comment I tore my shirt, pants, and boxers off, threw them to the side. She chuckled at the eagerness with which I followed her instructions. My cock curved upward in the afternoon light.

"Great," she said. "Now, you wouldn't mind if I undress as well, would you? I find I work best in the nude."

My mouth was dry as ash. I wet my lips, tried to get some moisture back into them. "No, uh, of course not. I don't mind."

With characteristic grace and dexterity, she unbuckled her jeans and curled them and her panties down to her ankles, lightly stepped out of them. I could see the pale, bare length of her legs, the supple thigh muscles that flexed underneath her smooth skin. And where those thighs met, the beautiful expanse of wild black curls. I thought I would come right there. I wanted nothing more than to bring my face to the meeting place of her thighs and breathe in the musky perfume.

She pulled her shirt off and I could see her flat stomach, her navel, the lace bra that held her two heaving breasts up. She turned away from me and I could not help but stare at her gorgeous ass, two masses of well-formed muscle.

"Would you mind unbuckling my bra for me?" she asked.

"Huh?" I shook myself out of my erotic reverie. "Oh, yeah, of course." I stepped forward and worked at the latch on her back. I struggled for a moment but managed to unclip it; but as I did so my massive erect cock accidentally brushed against the side of her hip.

"Sorry." I breathed.

She laughed a little, deep and throaty. Turned around and held my cock in her rough hand. "Don't apologize," she whispered, in teasing mimicry of my breathless voice.

"Your husband—" I started.

She cut me off. "Doesn't care."

"Is he—is he watching?"

She turned around, grinned at me. "Does it matter?"

I thought about it. I found I didn't care either way. She must have seen my decision on my face because before I could say anything she had already moved on. Taking her hand off my cock, she said, "I want you to pose like my wire mesh, can you do that?"

The wire mesh's body was angled as if about to turn to the side, or as if a lover were right over its shoulder. I attempted to mimic its pose, but Emily clucked in dissatisfaction. She knelt; I tried unsuccessfully not to think about how her face was right in front of my painfully erect cock. It was all I could do not to thrust forward so that my cock met her full lips.

She grabbed the flesh of my upper right thigh and moved my leg, took a step back and admired the change in my posture. She smiled in approval.

"There we go," she said.

She took a tool that looked like a long set of metal pincers from her table and began to hold it up to various parts of my body, altering how open the pincers were and then taking them to a sheet of paper on the table, comparing the opening widths to something and noting down what I could only assume were measurements.

"Are you measuring me?" I asked, hoping that a correct guess would impress her.

"Shh," she said, but flashed me a wink. "Yes, I am."

The last thing she measured was my cock. She whistled when she compared it to her chart on the table.

"You know your cock's eight inches long?" she asked.

"No," I said. I had never measured it before.

"I knew from the moment you were hard in your shorts that you were big, but eight inches..." She whistled again.

I had had a girlfriend my freshman year of college but she hadn't been any more experienced than me, so she hadn't had anything to compare my cock to either. I had always just assumed I was average. But I grasped from Mrs. Mirbeau's expression that eight inches was very, very large.

"You're thick too," she said, looking at her measurements but taking sneaking glances at my massive, erect cock. "Quite thick indeed."

Then Mrs. Mirbeau set to work, taking pieces of moist clay from a slab by her table and working them onto the mesh frame. She became lost in her work and began to assess my body with the eye of an artist, not aroused but appraising as she compared it to the work of her hands. She started with the feet and moved upward, not going into much detail but simply getting the basic shape in place, presumably to return to later.

At first I struggled to maintain my pose; but after a while, I became lost in the hypnosis of watching this beautiful naked woman work and the time began to fly by. Before I knew it, it was sunset.

As the dark surrounded us, Mrs. Mirbeau seemed almost to shake herself out of a trance. "I think that's enough for today," she said. "Would you mind coming back tomorrow? Earlier, perhaps?" She blushed slightly. "I had to put up the courage to come by your house, to be honest, or else I would have come by earlier. It never gets any easier to ask a new model to pose for me."

I let myself leave the pose, stretched my muscles. "I can't imagine anyone rejecting you, Mrs.—I mean, Emily."

She laughed and began to throw sheets of plastic over her work, to keep it moist I guess. It was only as she began to push it toward a shed that I realized she had it on a wheeled platform.

"Can you bring my clay block along?" she asked.

"Sure," I said, and picked up my boxers.

But she said, "No need to put on your clothes quite yet, Cameron." I couldn't tell for sure in the rapidly spreading darkness but it seemed that her eyes were sparkling with mischief.

So without any clothes on I heaved up the large brick of clay—it was even heavier than I expected, but I managed to stagger it into the shed where she had just wheeled her statue.

As I turned around to exit the shed, she grabbed my cock in her hand.

"You were rock hard that entire time, weren't you?" she whispered.

I didn't think I could manage words, so I just nodded to her.

"Well," she whispered, and she brought that beautiful face up close to mine, close enough that I could feel her bare breasts against my chest, I could smell the rose shampoo of her hair and the clay still on her body. "Why don't I help you out then?"

And she knelt in front of my cock like she did earlier, but this time she didn't leave it at that. She inspected my rock-hard, eight-inch long tool, stroked it a few times. She kissed the tip inquisitively. It was all I could do not to come at that moment. She laughed as my cock bobbed in frustration.

"Now, now," she said. "I know you've been waiting for the past three hours or so now, but you must understand that the best part about any carnal relation is the build up. We can't have you exploding just like that. Satisfaction requires patience."

So rather than returning her mouth to my cock she began to sprinkle light kisses on my thighs, on my lower stomach, and around the base of my cock, nonetheless avoiding the member itself. I moaned in frustration. She laughed again, against my skin; her warm breath tickled.

"Oh God, please—" I protested.

She put one hand against my stomach, in a gesture that somehow conveyed a command to quiet; so I did.

"Wait, wait," she said, not ceasing her soft kisses. "You must wait."

She began to lick my lower stomach; then, finally returning to my cock, she gave it a long lick from base to tip. I moaned.

She began to lap the head of my cock with her warm, wet tongue, looking up into my eyes periodically in the dim setting light and smiling.

And then, she submerged the head of my cock into her mouth, swirling her tongue around it.

Feeling her tight, hot, wet mouth around my cock was too much; I immediately came, yelling as I did.

I immediately felt ashamed and embarrassed. "Oh fuck, sorry," I said. "I know you said patience—" I didn't dare look at her, I was too terrified of the disappointment I would see.

But I felt her finger on my lips, silencing me. She had risen; in my shame I hadn't even noticed. I couldn't see any anger or disappointment in her eyes; only understanding.

Her expression made me suddenly daring—plus I wanted to make it up to her. "Let me eat you out," I said into her finger.

She seemed to consider this for a moment, then nodded. "Come this way," she said.

She grabbed a hold of my still erect cock and led me out of the shed, past her statue garden, and to a deck chair right by the back door.

Next to the door was a window; with a start I realized her husband, Mr. Mirbeau, was there. A second later and I realized he was naked as well, his hand on his own cock. He watched us with drooling arousal.

Mrs. Mirbeau lounged in the chair, opening up her legs so I could lower my face between them. "You're husband—" I said, pointing. I had already decided I was fine with him watching, but when I had thought about it, such an occurrence was theoretical; now that it was a fact, I was not put off, but I was put aback.

Mrs. Mirbeau turned around, smiled and waved. "Hey honey!" She looked at me. "I hope you don't mind?"

I shook my head. She leaned back in her chair, spreading her legs again; I didn't have to be told twice. I thrust my face straight into her sweet pussy, using my fingers to separate her thick bush and open up her engorged, already slick pussy lips.

Her pussy smelled good; it tasted good. Its musk made me even more aroused. My cock, barely slackened, shot back into its erection.

I licked her pussy lips, bottom to top; she moaned. "Oh yes," she said. "Yes yes yes."

I did it again; and then I thrust my tongue past her engorged pussy lips and into her cavity. She moved under me, as if trying to thrust her pussy farther along my tongue. I flicked my tongue in and out, then quickly brought it up to her engorged clitoris and licked it with the flat of my tongue.

"Oh God, yes," she shrieked. "You're good at that! Fuck!"

I continued my ministrations on her clitoris; she began to writhe under me. She wrapped her legs around the back of my head, tangled her fingers into my hair. She bucked against my tongue and lips.

Then, just as she seemed about to climax, she pushed my head away.

"I don't want to orgasm," she gasped. "Not yet." She grabbed my chin, stood up. "Get in the chair," she ordered.

Arousal had made her more authoritative than I expected. But I followed her orders, scrambling into the deck chair. She positioned herself so she was directly over my quivering, erect cock.

I was breathless; I was about to fuck the gorgeous Mrs. Mirbeau, in full sight of her husband.

She took my cock; rubbed it along her pink slit, against her engorged pussy lips and clitoris. Her pussy juices slid down my cock, making it slick. She closed her eyes as if allowing the sensation of my cock against her pussy to overwhelm her, as if any sensory detail beyond that would be too much for her to take. Then she pushed the head of my cock inside her and slid slowly down the massive erect length of my cock, one inch at a time.

"Fuck!" I yelled. It was like my cock was on fire, as if the fire were spreading down its length as her hot pussy engulfed me. On instinct my hands went to her hips, but when they did so, she grabbed them, pushed them up over my head.

She leaned down close to my face; her sweet breath tickled my nose. "No," she whispered. "I'm in charge, okay?"

She began to rock back and forth on my cock, slowly, grinding her clitoris against my pelvic bone.

I wanted to reach up with my lips and kiss her; but I didn't dare. I didn't dare do anything she didn't tell me to do. I just let her rock back and forth on my cock as I sat there.

Then she began to move up and down on my cock; it was all I could do not to gasp as her wet pussy slid up and down, releasing it to the cool night air before swallowing it back up again. Her breasts heaved up and down with each thrust.

Suddenly, she threw her head back, screamed. Collapsed on my chest. I could feel her pussy convulsing around the base of my cock; she was orgasming. I didn't think; the feeling was so exquisite I couldn't help but thrust upward, to come deep inside her.

"Fuuuuuuckkk!" I yelled.

It was only as I started to come down from the orgasmic heights that I realized what I had done; but before I apologized I realized she was purring against my chest.

"Delicious," she whispered. "My delicious stud."

I heard a ping against glass, something that sounded like a gasp. I looked over my head; Mr. Mirbeau had come as well, his cum a white streak on the window.

Mrs. Mirbeau kissed me, for what I realized was the first time. I kissed her back, hungrily.

"Don't forget," she said, "to come back tomorrow."

I wrapped my arms around her, felt her firm ass in my hands. No chance in hell I'd forget. "Of course, Emily," I said.